To Chris, my rock. —B.F.

To my cohorts from The Valley Forge—friends for life. —T.L.

The text of this book is set in Arquitecta. The illustrations were created using pencil,
watercolor, and colored pencil on Mi-Teites paper. Digital art assistance by Kristen Cella.

Library of Congress Cataloging-in-Publication Data Control Number 2014012651
ISBN: 978-0-544-03256-9
Manufactured in China SCP 10 9 8 7 6 5 4 3 2 1 4500511461
www.hmhco.com

STICK
AND
STONE

BETH FERRY

TOM LICHTENHELD

HOUGHTON MIFFLIN HARCOURT · BOSTON · NEW YORK

Stick.

Stone.

Lonely.

Alone.

A zero.

A one.

Alone is no fun.

Stick. Stone.

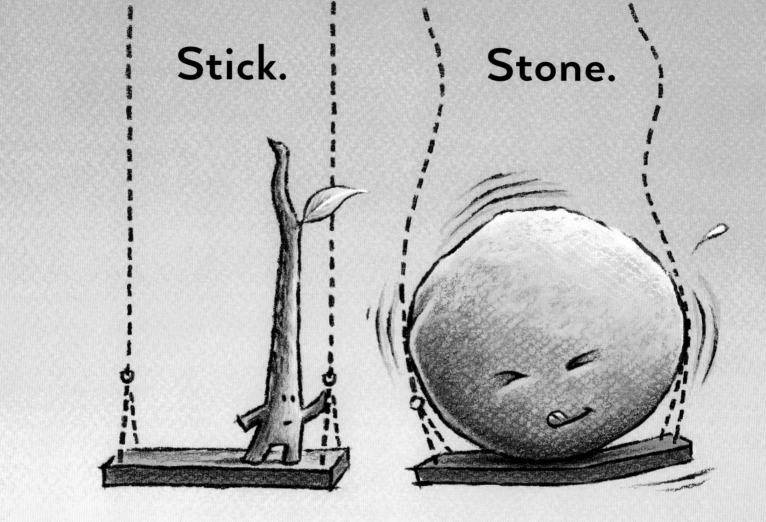

Along comes Pinecone.

Makes fun
of Stone.

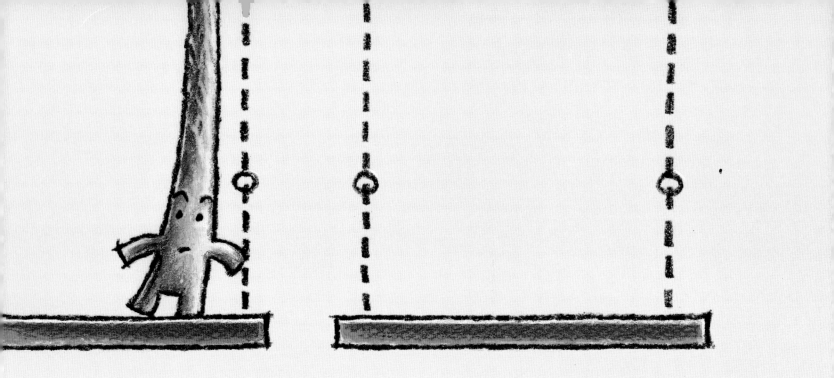

Won't leave
him alone.

"Vanish!" says Stick.

His word does the trick.

Stone whispers, "Gee, you stuck up for me!"

"That's just what sticks do. Friends do it too."

Stick,

Stone.

No longer alone.

Stick,

Stone.

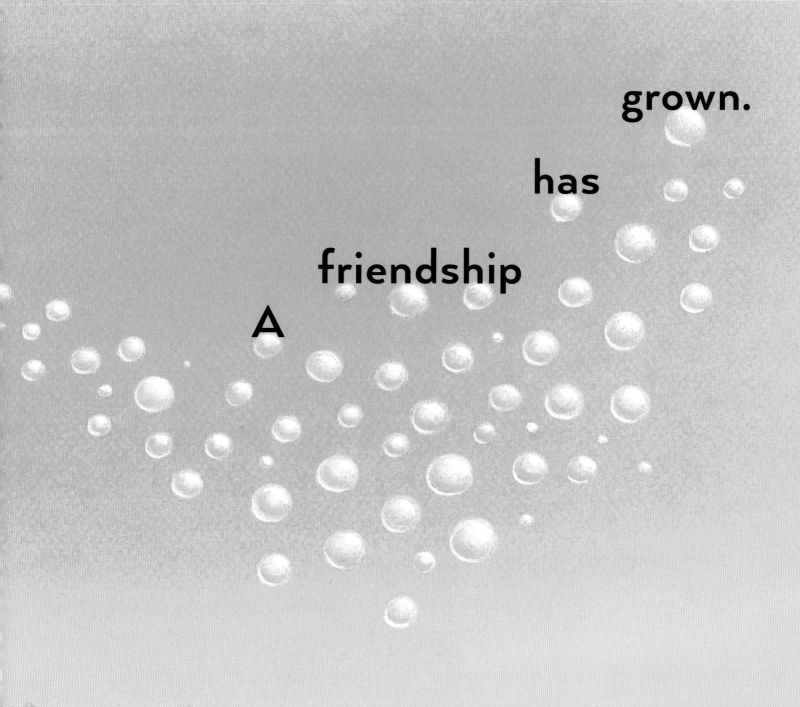

A friendship has grown.

They wander,

explore.

Laze by the shore.

Then thunder and rain,

Stick is windblown.

(There goes Pinecone!)

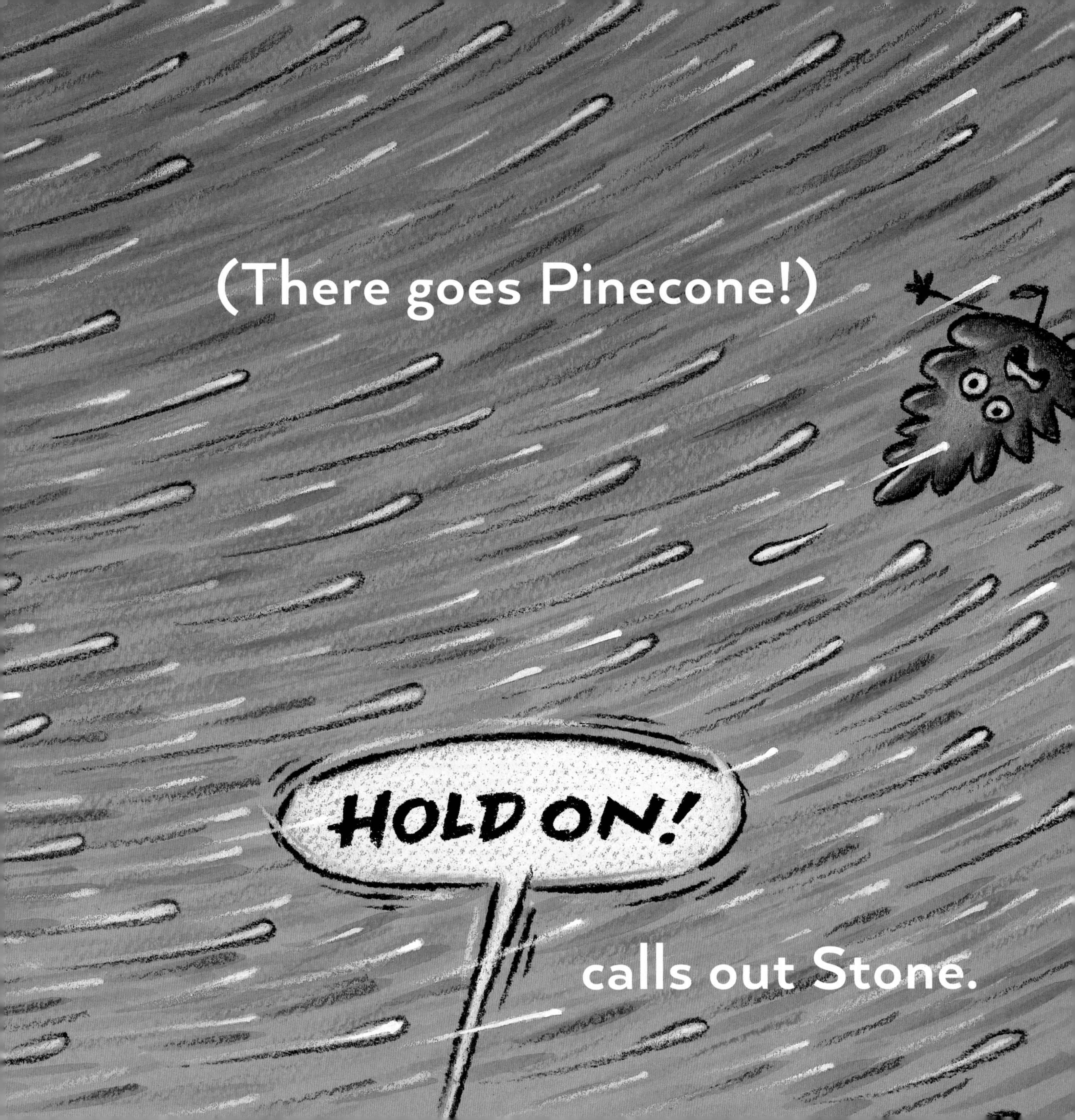

calls out Stone.

Again, he's alone.

and search night.

No Stick in sight.

What's this?
A huge puddle?

Stick stuck in the muddle.

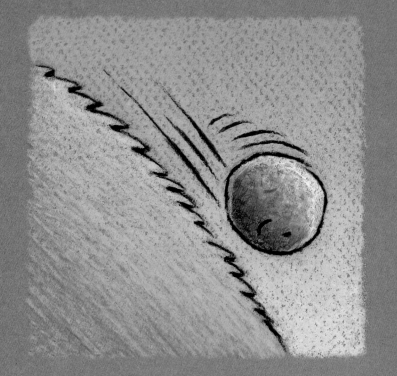

Stone rescues him quick.

"You rock, Stone," says Stick.

"That's just what stones do.
Best friendship rocks too."

Stick,
Stone.
Together again.

Stick,
Stone.
A perfect 10.

To The End.